Congratulations on choosing the best in educational materials for your child. By selecting top-quality McGraw-Hill products, you can be assured that the concepts used in our books will reinforce and enhance the skills that are being taught in classrooms nationwide.

And what better way to get young readers excited than with Mercer Mayer's Little Critter, a character loved by children everywhere? Our First Readers offer simple and engaging stories about Little Critter that children can read on their own. Each level incorporates reading skills, colorful illustrations, and challenging activities.

Level 1 – The stories are simple and use repetitive language. Illustrations are highly supportive.
Level 2 - The stories begin to grow in complexity. Language is still repetitive, but it is mixed with more challenging vocabulary.
Level 3 - The stories are more complex. Sentences are longer and more varied.

To help your child make the most of this book, look at the first few pictures in the story and discuss what is happening. Ask your child to predict where the story is going. Then, once your child has read the story, have him or her review the word list and do the activities. This will reinforce vocabulary words from the story and build reading comprehension.

You are your child's first and most influential teacher. No one knows your child the way you do. Tailor your time together to reinforce a newly acquired skill or to overcome a temporary stumbling block. Praise your child's progress and ideas, take delight in his or her imagination, and most of all, enjoy your time together!

Library of Congress Cataloging-in-Publication Data

Mayer, Mercer, 1943-
A yummy lunch / by Mercer Mayer.
p. cm. – (First readers, skills and practice)
Summary: Little Critter makes Mom his famous peanut butter, pickle, potato chips, and orange juice sandwich for lunch. Includes activities.
PB ISBN 1-57768-809-0
HC ISBN 1-57768-627-6
[1. Sandwiches—Fiction.] I. Title. II. Series.

PZ7.M462 Yu 2001
[E]—dc21 2001031210

Children's Publishing

Send all inquiries to:
McGraw-Hill Children's Publishing
8787 Orion Place
Columbus, OH 43240-4027

Printed in the United States of America.
PB 1-57768-809-0
HC 1-57768-627-6

1 2 3 4 5 6 7 8 9 10 PHXBK 06 05 04 03 02

A Big Tuna Trading Company, LLC/J. R. Sansevere Book

The McGraw-Hill Companies

FIRST READERS

Level 2 Grades K - 1

A YUMMY LUNCH

by Mercer Mayer

Columbus, Ohio

I am going to make lunch for Mom.
First, I need some bread.

GOOD
BREAD
GOOD
BREAD

Then, I need some peanut butter
to spread on the bread.

Then, I need some pickles to put on top of the peanut butter.

FRESH
OLD FASHIONED PICKLES

Then, I need some potato chips
to cover the pickles.

SPAGHETTI
SPAGHETTI
PASTA
ELBOWS
WHEELS
SAUCE
SPUD
BOY

FRESH
ORANGE
JUICE
S
P

Then, I need some orange juice
to pour on the potato chips.

CHIPS

“Mom! Lunch is ready. I made my famous peanut butter and pickle sandwiches with potato chips and orange juice!” I say.

P

I think Mom really likes her lunch. She says it is so good, that she wants to share it with Dad!

Word List

Read each word in the lists below. Then, find each word in the story. Now, make up a new sentence using the word. Say your sentence out loud.

<u>Words I Know</u>

bread
peanut butter
pickles
potato chips
orange juice

<u>Challenge Words</u>

going
lunch
ready
famous
sandwiches

How Does It Taste?

Pretend that you just tasted Little Critter's famous peanut butter and pickle sandwich. On a separate sheet of paper draw a picture of your face to show what it would look like. Then, write what you would say to answer Little Critter's question.

Action Words

Point to the action words below.

hug

dig

sandwich

dogs

run

Make a New Word

Use a separate sheet of paper for these activities.

Change one letter of the word fall to make a new word that goes with the picture.

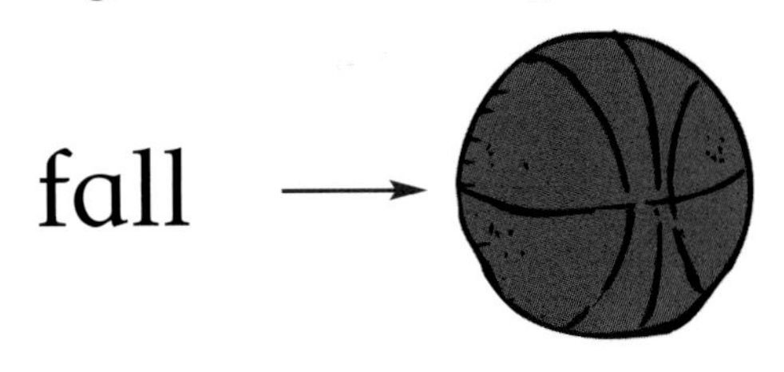

Change one letter of the word hug to make a new word that goes with the picture.

hug →

Change one letter of the word camp to make a new word that goes with the picture.

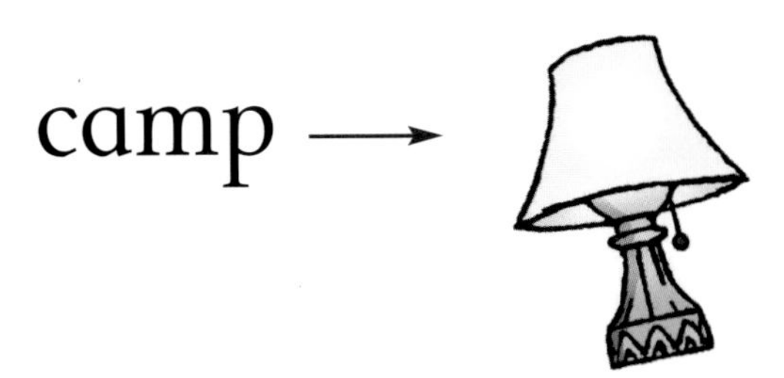

What Happened?

The food below is all part of Mom's sandwich. Point to each item in the order that Little Critter made the sandwich.

Word Families

Words come in word families. A word family is a group of words that has the same ending sound. Below are some words in two different word families. Add some more words to each word family. Use a separate sheet of paper.

day	top
say	pop
may	hop

Answer Key

page 19
How Does It Taste?

Answers will vary.

page 20
Action Words

page 21
Make a New Word

Change one letter of the word fall to make a new word that goes with the picture.

fall → ball

Change one letter of the word hug to make a new word that goes with the picture.

hug → bug

Change one letter of the word camp to make a new word that goes with the picture.

camp → lamp

page 22
What Happened?

2nd

page 23
Word Families

Sample answers given below.

hay	mop
bay	hop
pay	stop
ray	shop
lay	cop